Make A Wish Bear

by Greg Foley

SCHOLASTIC INC.

May your wish come true

Early one evening, a little bear
made a wish on a little star.

Bear sat and sat,
but nothing happened.

Mouse found Bear sitting alone.
"What are you doing?" she asked.
"I'm waiting for my wish to
come true," said Bear.

Mouse sat down to wait.

Soon Owl came by.
"We're waiting for Bear's wish
to come true," said Mouse.

"For a wish to come true," said Owl,
"you can't say it out loud."
"I didn't say it out loud," said Bear.
"Shhh," said Owl.

Then Fox walked up.
"We're waiting for Bear's wish
to come true," said Mouse.

"First you must close your eyes," said Fox.
So Bear closed his eyes.
"Cover them," said Fox.

Not long after, Elephant arrived.
"We're waiting for Bear's wish
to come true," said Mouse.

Elephant said,
"Try standing on one foot."
Everyone tried standing on one foot.

Pretty soon Turtle came along
and said, "If you hold your breath,
maybe it will come true."

"For how long?" asked Bear.

Then Bunny hopped up.
"What are you all doing?" he asked.

Bear looked around.
"If a wish already came true,"
he asked, "can you say it out loud?"

"Of course!" said Mouse.
"What was your wish?"

"To be together with all of you!"

ISBN 978-0-545-82953-3

12 11 10 9 8 7 6 5 4 3 2 1   14 15 16 17 18 19/0

Printed in the U.S.A.   40

First Scholastic paperback printing, December 2014

Set in American Typewriter Regular
The line art and color for this book were digitally rendered from pencil sketches.